I0621533

A Secret To Die For

Ghostly Tales From The Therapist's Couch

Matt Duff

First published in 2023 by Blossom Spring Publishing
A Secret To Die For. Ghostly Tales From The Therapist's Couch
Copyright © 2023 Matt Duff
ISBN 978-1-7394532-1-3
E: admin@blossomspringpublishing.com
W: www.blossomspringpublishing.com

In loving memory of my parents.
For my son James and wife Jemma for their
love and support.
For all my family, past and present.
Thank you for all your love and encouragement.

PROLOGUE – Ten years ago

"Good morning, Stan," said his secretary, Barbara. She was a short woman, around twenty-eight years old, with long blonde hair, tied up in a ponytail. She was dressed smartly as always. Barbara had been working for Stan for the last six years, ever since he'd been elected as an MP. They shared the same political beliefs and, therefore, had accompanied Stan on his election trail. Stan, after studying law and politics at university, had worked his way up the political ladder, and now, at thirty-five, had his own team and office in The House of Commons.

"Hi. Good morning, Barbara," Stan said cheerfully, while taking off his jacket and hanging it neatly on the hanger that was hooked on the back of his office door. Making his way to the swivel black leather chair located behind his large mahogany desk, he straightened his tie and sat down. A steaming mug of strong tea was already placed on the coaster to the right of him. Taking a careful sip, he sighed and visibly relaxed into his comfortable seat.

"Here's this morning's post. Mr Harris rang again. He wants you to call him back this morning," reported

Barbara.

"Thank you," he said, taking the pile of letters from her. Barbara returned to her own desk which was just a few feet away from her boss's office, on the other side of the door. As he sat forward, he began sifting through the pile of post to peruse their contents. One item was a brown internal envelope which he turned over. It was sealed and had the words top secret and confidential officially stamped on it but no name. Was it given to him by mistake? Curiously, he opened the envelope, removed the documents, scanned them and gasped, quickly replacing the contents back into the envelope. He picked up his mobile phone and dialled a number.

"Joe? It's Stan. Could you meet me at our usual place today? Half an hour?"

"Sure. No prob. Something wrong? You sound on edge," said Joe, concerned.

Hearing the hushed exchange, Barbara stopped typing and looked up from her keyboard.

"All's ok," he lied, upon seeing Barbara's concerned expression as he stuffed the envelope into his briefcase, grabbed his jacket with his spare hand and vacated his office. "See you later. Just popping out for an hour. I'll be back long before lunch." Stan hastily made his exit.

Joe had been friends with Stan ever since college. They had struck up a friendship with their interests in making a better world. Joe was a renowned journalist for a national newspaper. He was well regarded for his political commenting and had been interviewed on TV. In his political world, he endeavoured to remain neutral and so only expressed his newspapers opinions and not his own for fear of retribution. He'd had enough experience and foresight to know situations could very quickly change.

Joe was tall and slim, wearing blue jeans, trainers and a smart shirt. After his brief conversation with Stan, he donned his jacket, pocketed his phone, grabbed his bag with a camera in, which he went everywhere with, and left his office quickly. He had a nice office within a modern-looking glass building, which was a short walk to The House of Commons, and within easy reach of many underground stations. Joe arrived at the café first. It wasn't too busy for this time of day. A few tables and chairs were placed outside but Joe sat in. A selection of customers were scattered around, drinking their coffees, some eating delicious looking pastries, chatting intently.

Choosing a small round table in the corner by the window, he waited for his friend to appear. Stan duly arrived, having parked his car on the other side of the road, a short distance from the café. On entering, Joe smiled and waved him over. No sooner had they both taken their seats, a male waiter in a light blue shirt and wearing a dark blue apron with the coffee shop logo emblazoned on the front, came over to their table, and they ordered two coffees. Stan nonchalantly looked around before retrieving the envelope from his briefcase.

"This came to my office today. I must've received it by mistake," Stan said in a shaky, hushed voice as he nervously slid the envelope across the table, wearing a worried expression.

While Joe opened it, Stan furtively looked around the café again, mentally noting the occupants.

"So? Why don't you return it?" Joe said.

"Not as easy as that. Read the content."

Joe did so, and then looked up from the documents.

"Yeah. You're right. You can't return it."

"What should I do? You've got connections outside of politics, haven't you?"

"Leave it with me. I have an idea," Joe said

reassuringly.

Breathing a sigh of relief, Stan and Joe chatted while they drank, catching each other up and reminiscing. Drinks finished and with the envelope in Joe's satchel, they made their exit from the café into the street. Stan had offered Joe a lift back to the office. Just as they were about to cross the busy road, Joe realised he'd left his jacket on the back of his chair.

"My jacket. Be right back. I'll meet you at the car," said Joe, pointing back to where they just came from.

Stan nodded and crossed over the road to go to his car. As Joe was walking back outside, putting on his jacket, he looked up and saw his friend climbing into his car. As Joe began walking towards Stan's car, there was an enormously loud explosion that emitted a huge ball of flames which engulfed the car, setting off numerous car alarms nearby.

Joe was flung backwards to the floor. Passers-by lay bleeding where they fell. Those that were lucky, staggered away, clasping their ears, disorientated. Stunned, shocked and dazed, Joe slowly rose to his feet with constant ringing in his ears. He tried to get his breath back as he looked around in confusion. He saw the fire but didn't want to believe it was Stan's car. Then realisation dawned on him. Fighting back the instinct to help his friend, common sense and the instinct for survival kicked in. He hurriedly left the scene, sobbing convulsively.

On another corner of the street, a lone figure, dressed in black with a black rucksack slung over one shoulder, spoke into a mobile phone.

"It's done, boss."

"Good," came the monosyllabic reply. As the assassin put his mobile away, a very distressed looking man was rushing in his direction down the middle of the road. As he got nearer, the man in black noticed an envelope poking out the man's satchel. With the camera app on his phone, he quickly snapped a picture of Joe.

CHAPTER 1

Thomas habitually put his hands together as if in prayer and gazed out the window thoughtfully and reflected on his latest case. It was his way of thinking when sat at his desk in his tidy sizeable office for long periods of time — where he would make notes of his thoughts. Even just a fleeting thought would conjure up memories of past encounters and adventures. There were some that were harrowing and some that filled him with euphoria. When he wasn't making notes for an impending appointment to see his therapist, he would be writing about his ghostly exploits. He was fortunate to have a window with a panoramic view of luscious rolling hills, heather and tall pine trees where he could get lost in thought. His nearest neighbour was located just short of a mile away. He loved the isolation. In the distance, you could see a faint outline of the foothills of Ben Nevis. It was his and his families' idea of solitude. Remote and yet not far into the village of Kinlochleven to take his children to school and his wife, who worked in the local bakery, it was a short drive. It was a quaint village that had hardly changed in style over the decades. Shops and businesses were family run and had been for countless generations to ensure continuity which avoided decay. His office walls were adorned with photos of him receiving various accolades for his work such as police murder cases and grateful families for tracing deceased loved ones. On the wall facing his desk was a large landscape photo of himself, his children and wife posing, taken by a professional photographer. It was a happy scene and lifted Thomas whenever he encountered writers block or was between consulting appointments for his clients. Thomas's consulting room was adjacent to his office in an altogether separate wing of the detached house, far away from the chatter of his children and wife.

His foresight had showed him long ago he had a gift and that he could help others albeit whilst acknowledging his medium ability's negative side. It was a blessing and a curse at the same time. He could see and speak with the deceased and vibe from their negative energy. Clients would come to him from afar to be able to make contact with their departed loved ones. Using his business acumen, he started his medium consultancy when, as newlyweds, they moved addresses from the bustling urban sprawl of London to the vastness and panoramic scenery one could never tire of. Clients were far ranging in their vocations and experiences. His reputation had spread to many communities far and wide such was his respect for his client's privacy and dexterity to delve deeper.

Being a medium from such a young age was a double-edged sword for him. On the one hand, solving an age-old crime gave him and the police immense satisfaction, and, the bereaved closure. On the other, it could be fruitless with scant reward such as if a perpetrator had already died and which resulted in not getting the answers so longed for. In short, this fathomless ability was a blessing and a curse at the same time. So, some days he would feel good and invigorated, ready to take on the world, and others he would feel in a downward spiral. And it was because of these days he would make an appointment to see Ian Baker, his hypnotherapist, counsellor and friend, to offload his anxieties. Having developed a mind management plan, Thomas knew from experience when he would be in a downward spiral and thus would arrange an appointment before it got any worse.

His earliest recollection took him back to when he was

aged six. His mother and father were preparing him and his sister Nicola for bed. They were cleaning their teeth. Apart from his own reflection, he saw in the bathroom mirror another little boy, looking sooty and dishevelled. The boy's face, which was contorted in sadness and foreboding, looked forlornly at Thomas. Startled, Thomas wheeled round to the surprise of his parents asking was he ok. Their son, looking ashen and paralysed with fear, was reduced to whimpering noises. When the moment had passed, he was able to tell his parents what he had seen. To his surprise, his parents hadn't seen anything at all.

Taking a sip of his tea, Thomas thought about how worried and scared his mother and father had been for him. After another episode, his parents decided to seek professional help for him whereupon Thomas was declared a medium — after many long evaluations and tests. It was of paramount importance, the specialist told them, that he is treated as a normal child and has a normal childhood. Thus, as he grew up, he became laid back and had developed a balanced view of the world.

With the help of research and consulting his therapist, Thomas had grown more philosophical and understanding of the power he had. From a young age he had promised not to bury his negative emotions deep within himself (such was his foresight), and deal with those feelings, so he sought solace from Ian, his therapist, for emotional back up support and would relay to him, notes he had written that week. It was at the behest of Ian that Thomas began writing his memoirs as a form of self-therapy. Ian had been recommended to Thomas many years ago by the local police after becoming involved with Scotland Yard in a murder inquiry when he and his wife first got married.

*

As that memory faded his attention wandered to the photo on a shelf of him and his wife smiling while abroad on holiday. He looked at it fondly. Once again, he found himself reminiscing of how they first met.

Thomas had ordered an espresso from a coffee shop in Clapham and was waiting at the counter next to a well-presented but demure lady who was also waiting. The barista had given Thomas's coffee to the lady by mistake and the lady's order to Thomas. Neither of them realised until they exited the shop and started heading in the same direction. Thomas took a sip of espresso and discovered it had sugar and was frothy. He turned around to go back to the shop. The lady did the same too. It was only when they looked at each other, they realised they had each other's orders. They laughed and exchanged paper cups. Subsequent dates involved eating in nice restaurants and bars, movies in London's expansive West End, various museums, and their favourite, which was Covent Garden with its street performers, markets and cafes.

Back when Jemma and Thomas had first met, Jemma had been a tonic for him, taking him out of the doldrums of working at a book publisher which to him was a dead-end job. She was fascinated about his ability and the many tales he could tell. At the time, it wasn't a subject he would openly talk about unless asked. The more he spoke about dark subject matter, the lighter it became and he slowly began to realise that he could do something positive to help others.

Unbeknown to him, the other two people in the office at the publishers thought he was odd as he would stare into the distance from time to time. Little did they know that their office in this Victorian townhouse conversion had a ghostly visitor in the form of a young boy labourer. Michelle and Barry weren't aware that Thomas was absorbing and feeling this ghostly aura. Whenever Michelle and Barry had to go out of the office on business, Thomas would try to communicate with the apparition. When successful, he instantly found himself telepathically transported to another time. A tale he would recount vividly to his future therapist.

CHAPTER 2

Thomas felt he wanted to get away from it all and start a new life in different surroundings. Raise a family, write about his time travelling exploits, enjoy fresh country air. Before their children Amelia-May, Catherine and James were born, most weekends the two of them would venture into the foothills of Ben Nevis and marvel at its vast open barren plains, save for a few beautiful, serene lakes and an abundance of wildlife. Sometimes, you could hear the call of a golden eagle if you were lucky and see them acrobatically perform, or a deer or two, providing you were furtive. It was the perfect place to go rambling and chance upon an inn for refreshment and food.

As he gazed out the window whimsically making notes to tell his therapist, another flashback came to him and once again he felt himself lost in memories.

*

It was out on a rambling expedition with Jemma before the children were born, that they encountered a crime scene marked by a tent, police tape and official looking personnel. Thomas had liaised with forensic teams in the past. An incident had occurred the day before, and evidence was still being examined, investigated and then cross examined. The constable on duty put his hand up and told them to not to come any further and was reluctant to give any details about what was going on when asked. Suddenly, Thomas went motionless and stared through the forensic team around the tent. The constable said again to be on their way. Upon recognising Thomas's body language, Jemma reassured the constable, who seemed to instantly relax. This was going to turn out to be one of his most interesting and involved cases that wasn't what it seemed at first glance. To be the bearer of weighty information as this, and knowing it to be a national security issue, was the heaviest burden he had ever had.

*

Hastily, Thomas made more notes before he would have to get ready to leave for the picturesque walk along a winding lane through the village and just beyond. He looked forward to the walk as it was a time to gather his thoughts while he savoured the fresh air and admired the scenery. Just then, his office door was flung open, and in bounded his three children, James, Catherine and Amelia-May.

"Are you ready to take us to school, daddy?" one said as they hugged him.

"I sure am. I'll just get my coat."

They all entered the hallway and put on their coats. His wife Jemma finished her toast as she put on her coat over her work apron.

"Mummy, could you bring home some muffins from the bakery, please?" asked James.

"Of course. Chocolate chip I presume," Jemma replied.

"Yes please," chorused all three children.

Turning to Thomas, Jemma said, "Say hi to Ian from me and remember to tell him about that old case of yours you keep dreaming about."

Thomas opened their front door and they all headed out. After saying goodbyes, Jemma climbed into her car to head for the local bakery where she worked, while Thomas and the children set off down the road towards the local primary school.

CHAPTER 3

Admiring the passing scenery, Thomas finally made his way down the quiet, residential street where Ian lived. It was in the middle of the picture postcard village in the foothills of Ben Nevis that they both shared. The sun was shining and a warm breeze tickled his neck. As he approached the large, detached house, he stopped at the large, black ornate gate with its sign declaring "Ian Baker – hypnotherapist". Looking up, he was surprised to see the gates already open and Ian standing in the doorway, ready to greet him.

"Good morning, Thomas," said Ian who extended a hand which was followed by a hearty handshake.

"Good morning," Thomas replied and was promptly shown into Ian's therapy room at the furthest end of his house. He was immediately offered coffee as usual. Thomas settled himself on the couch. In front of him was a small, rectangle wooden coffee table. It was a pleasing room with its light magnolia coloured walls, soft, deep pile light brown carpet and cosy décor and furnishings which gave such a meeting a relaxed ambience. Scented candles stood on shelves around the room, ready to be lit to fragrance the air and help soothe harrowing sessions. Large bay windows with magnificent views gave the individual a choice of letting in more light or not with the aid of full-length patterned curtains in various shades of calming soft colours.

Ian presented the coffee and put the mug on a table next to Thomas while they had their usual light-hearted chat first. Before the conversation started to turn serious, the mug was removed and replaced with a glass of water. Revisiting memories often became traumatic when told with such vividness that the orator became parched. Also, on the table was a box of tissues. He sat across the other side of the room to Thomas on a single swivel chair poised with a notepad and pen.

"Okay, Thomas. Begin when you're ready and at your own pace." Ian sat quietly patient while Thomas readied himself and perused his notes. A few seconds passed until Thomas was ready to speak.

"I had another flashback this morning of that scene by the railway line when I was rambling with Jemma all those years ago. Do you remember me telling you?" asked Thomas.

"Ah, yes I do," Ian replied interestedly.

There was a long pregnant pause while Thomas steeled himself and tried to remember everything he could manage so as to unburden himself. Ian knew this could take a while from his previous sessions with Thomas and was therefore happy to wait, as he appreciated his psychic abilities and had never met anyone like Thomas before. Ian's usual clients were those that required regression or hypnotherapy for deep seated emotional problems. But Thomas, he found fascinating.

"I felt an overwhelming feeling of despair, sadness and surprise. Panic, too. But, not from one presence. There were *two*. There had been a struggle with another man. This man had been ordered to kill someone that they were supposed to be protecting. These two men were murdered by the assassin."

Thomas was clenching the sides of the couch tighter now while all the time staring unfalteringly into the distance at the hills. Ian looked aghast at this revelation and was hastily making notes. Thomas paused while he readied himself to delve deeper.

"What I am about tell you is traumatic."

Not knowing what response he should give, Ian calmly said, "Okay," even though he looked nervous.

Although Thomas had his eyes open, Ian knew from Thomas's many visits that Thomas was 'in the memory' and not seeing him. Ian took this opportunity to reach for his own glass of water.

"These were two young detectives from Scotland Yard who were guarding a reporter who was told a secret that could harm national security. They were taking him to a safe house."

Ian looked more aghast and intrigued and nearly dropped his pen as the memories came flooding back for Thomas. He gripped it tightly for fear that any noise could bring Thomas out of this state. Tears began to roll down Thomas's cheeks as he understood why the two detectives were sad and in despair. They were both married and had young families. This was something both Thomas and Ian could relate to. Shakily and absent-mindedly, Thomas reached for a tissue.

"There is something my ability allows me to do which I haven't told you about before," stated Thomas. "You already know that I can sense and see things when I touch an object related to the person or scene. When I have a vision, it is like being transported back in time to the actual event, like I'm really there. If I am touching someone when this happens, I am able to take them with me so they can also experience the vision and see for themselves." Thomas gave Ian a moment to digest this information. "Is this something you would be happy to try?"

"Is it dangerous?" asked Ian, looking a bit worried.

"No, there is nothing to be afraid of," replied Thomas, shaking his head. "No one we encounter can hear or see us. We are not affected by the events that take place and are unable to make any changes. What has happened has happened. Be aware though, that some things you may see could be unpleasant or frightening."

After a pause, Ian said, "Okay, I'll do it!"

As he was about to continue, Thomas sank further back into the couch and beckoned for Ian to come closer. Not knowing if he should, curiosity got the better of him and did as he was bade, rolling his chair around so he was positioned next to the end of the couch where Thomas was sitting.

"Is it ok if I place my hand on your arm? There has to be physical contact for me to take you with me," Thomas asked. Ian nodded his assent.

Thomas placed his hand on Ian's right forearm. Ian

heard a strange whooshing sound and unexpectedly, found himself transported to another time.

CHAPTER 4

Ian suddenly found himself in the middle of a mud filled field. Thick, black clouds blanketed most of the sky, almost completely concealing the moon. Yet, he could see everything clearly. The smells that bombarded his nostrils told him he was in the countryside. Lashing rain struck the already soaked ground all around him, causing the already huge ditches to continuously overflow with muddy water. Thomas stood beside him. However, they themselves were unaffected by the weather. Neither the torrential rain or the howling wind could touch them. Nor did they feel the biting chill of the night.

"What's happening?" said Ian, looking confused and stumbling about.

"It's okay. Trust me!" reassured Thomas, placing a hand on Ian's shoulder. "We're perfectly safe." Ian held out his hands as if trying to feel the rain that seemed not to affect them.

Suddenly, in the distance, Thomas noticed a lone, ragged, running figure, occasionally looking over his shoulder, silhouetted against the odd moon beams that managed to penetrate the dark clouds, trampling on ferns and hurdling stiles. Seeing this figure running and the state it was in, it was obvious it was fleeing. And by the sheer panic etched on its face, it became apparent it was a distressed man whose breathing was rapid and laboured. They carried on observing this desperate sight. "We need to follow him," stated Thomas. "And remember, we are only observers. We can't interact with these events or change anything. The past is the past."

*

The rain was relentlessly drumming on Joe's already thoroughly soaked scalp, which depressed him even further, all the while he was trying to flee across this hopelessly dark field. His feet felt like they were sloshing around in his shoes having absorbed so much from all the muddy puddles he'd stepped into.

Finally, street lights came into view in the distance and shone down on the recently ploughed ground. Upon seeing this, his spirits lifted, and with renewed vigour, staggered up an embankment to the edge of the road. He whirled around to check if he had been followed. There were no sounds and no signs of torch lights either. He was safe he hoped. Upon realising this, he searched his mind as to why he had been running and how he came to be here. It all happened so fast, he was finding it hard to focus. From taking in his surroundings, he got a vague idea of his location. "But how did I get here?" he pondered. He now knew he had some unexplained gaps in his memory. His panting slowed, but his heart was still racing.

To gather his thoughts, he sought a place to sit and recover and spied an empty bus shelter with a bench. In the distance, across the hilly road, he noticed more street lights populated with houses and other buildings. "A town centre," he assumed. He looked up and saw a bus timetable poster to his side. The terminus was Glencoe.

"Glencoe? I'm in Scotland! How did I get here?" he said incredulously.

His head was again whirling. This time it was with disbelief, shock and so many unanswered questions. A metallic white saloon car with a taxi company name scribed down the length of its side, pulled up and a cheerful looking fellow in his mid to late 50s wearing a thick maroon coloured jumper and a flat cap lowered a window, and said loudly, in a local dialect, to be heard over the rain, "The last bus has gone, mate."

"I don't need a bus. Actually, I'm not sure *how* I

got here."

Upon seeing this dishevelled and soaking wet person, who clearly wasn't local by his accent, the driver replied, "Must have been a great party."

"No. Nothing like that," Joe shook his head.

"I'd like to give you a ride, but I've finished for the evening."

Just then, the sheltered man had a jolt of realisation. "Lights. I remember bright lights. And a train?" Joe rubbed his head and looked puzzled.

The driver looked quizzically back at the wet man, who stared vacantly into the distance, as if having a flashback. "Are you alright?" he asked. The driver quickly came to the realisation that the man genuinely needed help and wasn't a drunken reveller after all.

"I just need somewhere to sit and think," Joe responded.

"Hop in. I'll take you to The Railway Tavern. You could get a coffee and use the phone, too. It's right next to the train station," said the driver as he reached over to open the passenger side door.

"Thanks. That would be great." The man climbed in the front passenger side of the taxi and locked his seatbelt in place.

*

Thomas and Ian were now taking shelter at the bus stop, for all the difference it made. "How are we going to follow them now?" asked Ian, as he watched the taxi pull away.

Just as Thomas was about to answer, they heard a strange whooshing sound and suddenly they both found themselves in the back of the taxi. A shock expression settled on Ian's face. Thomas just smiled. This wasn't his first trip into the past. Getting comfortable, both men sat listening to the conversation playing out in front of them.

*

"Won't they be closed at this time of night?"

"No. They always have a lock in on a Friday. It's common knowledge with the locals. Besides, the nearest police station is at Loch Laggan — miles away."

"Oh right. Friday? Did you say Friday?"

"Yes. That's right. You don't look so good."

Immediately, he delved into his coat pocket. His hand was met by a vacant space. "My phone! It must have come out of my pocket when I was running!" Turning to the taxi driver, Joe asked, "Has anything big happened in the news today or yesterday?"

"No. Usual political shit. Just more of the same. Here we are, then. The Railway Tavern."

"Thanks for the ride. Can I buy you a coffee?"

"Sure. I'll tell my good lady I had a late fare. Besides, you'll need me to get you in, because they won't open their doors to strangers."

"Thanks for the lift. I'm Joe," he said as they shook hands.

"Good to meet you. I'm Pat."

CHAPTER 5

The scenery changed yet again and images flashed by and were replaced. Now Ian and Thomas found themselves inside the tavern, standing in one corner and could hear the low hubbub of drinkers huddled together in groups so as to keep hushed talk to a minimum and observed the immediate surroundings. Arched brick walls adorned with various copper and brass antiquities. The fireplace created an entertaining spectacle of constantly dancing flames punctuated by its crackling noises. They both relaxed a little upon feeling the convivial ambience and continued closely watching the two men for answers.

The two newly acquainted men were sat at a small round table. The only light was from people's mobile phones and a side room with a dimmer switch which was turned nearly all the way down. To the outside world it would appear that sordid goings on of the carnal kind would be in full swing, the tavern was that dimly lit and quiet. Little did the outside world know the town's whiskey drinkers were having secret "wee" drams.

By now, Joe was nearly dry so Thomas and Ian both inferred that a little time must have passed. Joe seemed revived enough to begin to try and answer his own questions from earlier with the help of the local dram.

"How's the whiskey, Joe?" Pat said warmly, having got into the spirit of the lock in with a couple of quick drams himself.

"Fantastic stuff. I can see why the locals like a lock in."

"What were these bright lights you were talking about?" asked Pat, looking thoughtful.

"I'm trying to remember."

"You also asked if anything had happened in the news. What's going on? Are you in any trouble?"

Pat had had a longing for mystery and adventure his whole life. As a kid, he had a great imagination and often travelled to unknown worlds, had undersea adventures or fought off pirates with his younger brother at his side. At times, he found himself pining to get away from the everyday routine of picking up the usual fares, visiting the usual places, passenger's overpowering odours, familiar routes and telling him about their day, which he considered more hum drum than his own.

He had had an enjoyable career in the distillery industry since he left college and gained an interest in glassware from an art project as a student. The young Pat was fascinated by the shapes and patterns that could be made using glass. Particularly vibrant and rich colours. This led to an interest in glass blowing in a decade long before bottles and conveyor belts had an automated style of production. Based at Fort William, in a whiskey distillery, he graduated through different stages of the production process to Chief Foreman before he was untimely made redundant with lots of other staff, as a result of a takeover by a foreign distillery company.

As Joe began to gather his thoughts, memories came rushing back to him in a disassembled jumbled state. He recalled dark images and outlines of trees and hedges that bordered the field he ran across. Particularly, the unrelenting drumming sound of rain. As if jolted by an electric shock, Joe remembered hearing a man's voice in the distance. Joe didn't see him but recognised the accent as American. To be more precise, the voice was of a Brooklyn dialect.

"You look shocked. I'll get us another round of whiskey, Joe," Pat said cordially, excited and intrigued all at the same time.

Joe nervously scanned the bar saloon and games area

upon beginning to realise why he had been running and why he was here. He was starting to remember more now. He noticed that all the other patrons were not looking at him anymore and had continued with what they were doing. He felt himself relax.

Pat returned with two whiskies. "You look like you're more calm now. That'll be the local dram working its charm. Is there anything I can do to help?"

"I'm not sure. I'm having trouble remembering clearly and piecing everything together. I keep getting flashes of memory, but they don't make sense. I think I bumped my head," responded Joe, rubbing the back of his head.

"Tell me what you can remember and we'll try to figure this all out."

Ian and Thomas looked at each other and recognised that the man had indeed remembered something.

*

Back in Ian's home, feeling the suspense, Ian gripped the seat of his chair harder. The grip that Thomas had on Ian's forearm remained the same albeit each other's sinews were now more alert.

CHAPTER 6

So intent were Thomas and Ian at trying to listen to this secret conversation, that when the scenery once again whizzed by like life flashing before one's very eyes, it was clear the same thoughts were running though their minds. Where are we going now? And, we need to hear this conversation! When they had settled and the surroundings were static, they found themselves back again in the same muddy field as before but with a new person. Both looked at each other in surprise to be back where they started. They watched and followed.

*

A bright circle of light shone on the floor in the field and swayed from left to right as if searching. The source looked like it was hovering a few feet off the ground and therefore gave itself away as a torch. A silhouette was behind the torch and was surveying the ground, occasionally crouching down. The intensity of the rain had eased but it was clear the new addition to this adventure was soaked through too. The inspection of the ground was suddenly interrupted by a trill from the man's coat pocket. The man grabbed his phone from his coat pocket.

"Well? Is the job done?" said the caller before the man could even say a word.

"No. He got away. But don't w-"

"You idiot! That's twice now you've failed. The only reason I put up with you is because you're family. But that can change. I want it done! Don't let me down! No loose ends! Call me when it's completed!" demanded the South American voice.

"You got it," promised the chilling voice of the assassin.

Ian looked incredulously at Thomas and now realised that this man was probably the reason the other man was running through this very field only a short time ago. This guy was after him. But why?

*

As the assassin was wanted for numerous assassinations around the world of political figures, cartel rivals and just about anyone that stood in the way of his employer, he was given to use many aliases or code names. He was always paid handsomely and had been for a few decades since he embarked on this career path. His many talents saw him in high demand from the underworld and their cosy connections with governments and regimes around the world. He could change his accent and spoke many languages, blending into many a scene with the greatest of ease before doing what he was paid to do and leaving no trace. He enjoyed the luxury he was afforded, the fear in which he was held and the anonymity of it all. He'd come a long way from serving his country which sometimes meant stealth attacks of one kind or another. Abseiling speedily and silently from rooftops, long range sniping in daylight or darkness. Above all, he relished the hunting of his victims. The feeling of exhilaration had never left him. Even when his troop were disbanded by the U.S. government on completion of their last mission, which was utter suicide and, of course, kept secret from the U.S. public.

Rico discovered a partly crushed knee-high bush that had recently been fallen onto. He then spied a wet mobile phone covered in mud. It was in a puddle. A puddle formed by a person's body. Unluckily for Rico, the battery was dead before it hit the ground. No amount of charging would bring it back to life as it was thoroughly waterlogged. The one confirmed clue he did find were footprints. Upon close examination, he saw that the impressions were heaviest where the toes would have been, indicating beyond doubt this person was running. He followed the runner's trail to the roadside where they were beginning to not be so clear. Rico picked up the faint trail a little further along, heading towards a bus shelter where they were no more. Completely vanished. It didn't make sense. Buses stopped running hours ago. Why else come to a bus shelter if not for cover at time of night and in the rain, but then where do you go? Just then, he caught a glimpse of a muddy partial fingerprint on the glass fronted frame of the bus timetable.

He put himself in the runner's shoes and tried to guess where he would go to next. Which direction? Rico looked in one direction and his phone's GPS gave away no possibilities. He faced the other direction and stood still allowing his eyes time to adjust to the partly unlit road. In the distance, he saw a faint cluster of lights. Street lights? A village, perhaps? He checked the GPS on his phone and it seemed very likely the runner would have headed in that direction.

Ian looked at Thomas with a concerned look on his face.

"If he enters the pub, Joe will be discovered. Surely

there must be something we can do. Warn him in some way!" exclaimed Ian.

"I'm sorry Ian. This is the past. The events are fixed. There is nothing we can do other than watch them play out. Hopefully, what we learn here will help me heal the souls of those left behind and those souls having trouble passing on," explained Thomas.

Now, understanding a bit more about what was happening and what they were seeing, they both became more and more intrigued as they found themselves back in the saloon bar of the pub again.

The TV above the bar was showing a story about a well-known journalist from a leading British national newspaper who had gone missing in suspicious circumstances. The TV displayed earlier interviews outside the head office of the national newspaper with colleagues who were clearly baffled, bewildered and generally concerned for their well-loved journalist's welfare. Joe's picture appeared on the screen. Despite the TV being mute and displaying subtitles, it spoke volumes about the gravity of the situation.

Joe saw the TV screen out of the corner of his eye and immediately stopped whispering to Pat and became transfixed on the screen which now showed a police officer being interviewed. Pat's gaze followed Joe's. He turned away from the TV to face Pat, his face showing helplessness, desperation and panic all rolled into one.

"I'd better get you another wee dram of the good stuff," said Pat reassuringly and promptly rose, patting Joe's shoulder as he walked past him to the bar.

Pat returned with new drinks, placed them on the table and sat down.

"Cheers. You're a good man, Pat," Joe said as they clinked glasses together.

CHAPTER 7

In London, the missing journalist was the top story in national newspapers, on radio and TV. Due to the wide reporting, speculation was rife as to why he was missing. One national newspaper even posed the question, "Is missing journo held hostage?"

On the instruction of the police and senior detectives, and as with any witness protection, Joe was unable to tell anyone what had happened or where he was being taken, not even his editor and friend George Peters. Also, what nobody knew was Joe's current situation — fleeing. Previous scoops and stories were being looked into by work colleagues for clues as to why Joe had disappeared. He hadn't been into the office for some days, he wasn't answering his phone and he wasn't at home. What did he know that could put him in danger? Had he uncovered a can of worms? Staff were interviewed by George, one by one. Emails were trawled through. His weekly column was replaced with a guest writer until the situation was clearer. Due to his popularity, Joe had appeared on TV satire panel game shows and was sometimes sought for his respected opinion and experienced insight into the sometimes publicly perceived banal and murky political world. Joe had a good reputation for knowing a good scoop and how to report it. As much as he was witty, he was never scathing. He was all too aware that politics could bite back at any time. He was popular with many MP's. Opposition or not, he'd had many a lunch time meal, pint or coffee. MP's trusted Joe because they knew that if what they said to him was stated as "off the record," then it remained that way and was not made public. Lunch meetings were just that. Lunch meetings. Like-minded people with mutual interest and the ability to see the bigger picture in the political world and see through deception for political gain.

*

The door handle creaked menacingly and then remained motionless. A silhouette stayed still as if waiting. The shadow's head became larger as it neared the glass in the door as if to listen. A collective hush descended inside the inn. For some, it heralded an impromptu police presence. For two patrons it represented fear of another kind. The silhouette then made a sign with his fingers. The barman watched intently at the sign made against the window. He promptly opened the door which then creaked as if to add to the building suspense. Joe prepared to bolt having already spied a rear door.

"Come in, Bernie. We were wondering if you would come tonight," whispered the landlord.

"Couldn't get away. There was a suspected intruder in the yard. Never found anyone though and nothing missing. Probably another moose," he said nonchalantly.

Upon realising, it was just another late drinker, there was a collective sigh of relief. Particularly, from the teller of a secret that could potentially harm the nation's international trading reputation, security and it's standing on the world stage. Fellow drinkers smiled and raised their glasses at him.

Bernie was a security guard at a timber yard near the foothills of Ben Nevis where it was heavily wooded. Hunters frequented the area for deer, but, mostly moose. It was a popular hunting ground for birds of prey, particularly eagles of one kind or another. As the birds were a protected species, rangers were often seen patrolling with conservationists who kept up to date numbers of the many species and their movements. Often after the hunters had gone, foxes and other scavengers foraged for rich pickings that were either leftovers from the hunter's lunch or the quarry itself. Some hunters came at night in complete darkness, armed with silenced rifles and infra-red binoculars and telescopic sights. It wasn't uncommon for nocturnal creatures to forage there either. The reason silenced rifles were used was anonymity as the purchase of a licence was very costly. Infra-red cameras and motion sensor cameras were strategically placed high up on tree trunks as sentinels for bats residing in specially adapted boxes and protected birds' nests, giving live feeds to conservationists in expertly camouflaged cabins dotted around the foothills. From there, the object of the camera could be monitored without intrusion, movements logged and, in spring, hatchlings observed for their wellbeing. Buzzards and eagles liked the vast expanse and openness of the mountainous area that is Ben Nevis. A place where they can glide and soar and not encroach on other birds' territory. With rolling hills, babbling streams that meandered for miles in abundance, nature's food larder was ever plentiful. As with all mountainous regions in Scotland it was a popular destination for hikers, mountaineers who wanted to bathe in its majesty and bird watchers to revel in birds' acrobatic feats of agility in a splendid panoramic background. As for photographers and painters, they wanted to capture its majesty and marvel at its gloriousness for all time.

Joe had a vastly superior knowledge of politics and more experience than anyone on his newspaper. He had acquired and honed the ability to read between the lines of what political figures said and what they meant and ultimately, their true goal as well as what they stood to gain. In essence, he had built a mental profile of all MP's and got introduced to new ones too. Therefore, he knew who he could and couldn't trust. A word he had stood by and seen him through many political scoops and stories.

He had an advantage that a lot of his opposite number journalists on other newspapers didn't have. He had been at university with a lot of current MP's and so had formed long-standing bonds over many a drink and dinner party, and subsequent reunion parties. There was one friend he did a lot of fun things with like rambling, mountaineering and orienteering, particularly in National Parks at weekends. Stan Meacher. How he missed Stan. His mind flooded with images from that fateful day and events up to now. As if waking from a bad dream he emitted an audible shudder.

"That whiskey sure does the trick on a horrible night like this, eh?" Pat said emphatically and raised his glass. "What were you trying to tell me, laddie?" sensing adventure.

They huddled closer over their table once more to exchange whispers. Joe surveyed the room carefully for any listeners, obviously unaware of Thomas and Ian standing close by. Satisfied, he turned to Pat while thoughtfully swilling the "wee dram".

Joe told Pat about the car bombing, his friend Stan and the envelope.

"I'm sorry about your friend," consoled Pat.

"If I'd got into the car too, I wouldn't be here either!" A single tear rolled down his cheek. "Someone's after me because of what I know. He tried to kill me."

CHAPTER 8

Aghast at being told this, Pat's jaw dropped and realised this really was happening. He gestured to Joe to pause while he absorbed this news. He took Joe's now empty glass and returned with two replenished glasses. Their eyes didn't leave each other.

Joe continued to recount his story. He cast his mind back and immediately was lost in thought unaware he was narrating what he recalled.

"I was given advice by the police and Home Office after I was interviewed to go to a safe house in Scotland. They kept me there for ages then eventually a Senior Detective Draper from Scotland Yard came in. He said I was lucky to be alive and had stumbled into the middle of a highly sensitive situation. We boarded a sleeper train from St Pancras to Glasgow. I was given two undercover detectives to travel with me but he must have found out. He killed them too." Pat was incredulous and raised his glass in astonishment once more.

"What? So, this killer follows you onto the train?" Pat said in disbelief.

"Yes. He must've known I hadn't seen his face. Why

else would he befriend me?"

"You're kidding."

Joe was immediately taken back to the scene as he described to Pat the events that led up to the assassin's attempt on his life and his near escape.

Thomas and Ian listened, enthralled.

Thundering along with the occasional click clack. The vast openness of the countryside. Distant deer grazing but their form unmistakable. Brown and well trampled ferns. Vibrant colours of heather and flax. The freshness of the air in his nostrils from the open window. A whoosh of wind passing through his hair. Momentarily, Joe found himself alone in his seat at the end of the carriage, all three of their bags stowed on the overhead rack. Detective Mitchell had gone off to get some refreshments from the buffet carriage further down the train. However, when he failed to return, the other detective, Noonan, said he needed to see what was taking so long and told Joe to stay put. The train wasn't that busy. A few other passengers were seated around tables further up, some clearly travelling for business, smartly dressed, tapping away on their lap tops, others listening to music or chatting on their phones to friends and loved ones. Joe heard the sound of approaching footsteps and looked up from his newspaper. Standing before him was a cleanshaven slender looking man about 5' 10" tall, short brown hair in his mid-thirties Joe guessed. He had on black jeans, a plain red top and black jacket with a ruck sack slung over his shoulder.

"Mind if I sit here?" said the man and quickly sat down opposite Joe before he was able to respond. The stranger continued to talk, without pausing for breath, giving Joe no opportunity to protest. Although nervous at first, the more the man talked about his life, the more relaxed Joe became. Just an ordinary chap looking for company Joe assumed. Talk turned to the reason for his trip which included walking and bird watching around Ben Nevis. Joe, who was also an avid bird watcher, was finally able to contribute to the conversation. The man gave a sniff and his hand reached into his jacket pocket, as if looking for a tissue, and the next thing Joe knew, he was looking down the barrel of a gun. Having no choice, Joe was forced to make his way along the corridors that ran the length of the carriages to the back of the train.

Looking around at the other passengers they passed, Joe wondered if there was something he could do or say to help the situation. As if reading his mind, the stranger said, "Don't even think about it. You wouldn't want anyone else to get hurt, would you?" Joe just kept walking.

In the last section of the train was a separate space with an emergency door. The assassin told Joe to open it. Joe reached for the handle, hoping the alarm would go off, alerting the guard that help was needed.

"Don't worry about the alarm," said the assassin, having seen Joe notice the "in case of emergency" instructions. "I've already dealt with that earlier. Useful door this."

Joe felt a sudden surge of adrenalin as reality of death loomed. The ground seemed nearer. He gripped the sides of the door way as he felt the hard metal of the gun press into his back. Without warning, the train speed suddenly decreased, surprising both parties, causing the assassin and Joe to stumble back, falling in a heap on top of each other.

"Shit!" thought Rico as he banged his head on the hard steel floor and knocked himself out. Stumbling to get back on his feet, Joe stood next to the now still man. A million thoughts raced through his mind. Was the man dead or just unconscious? He had to get away. He couldn't risk returning to his carriage, even if it meant leaving his bag behind. At least he had his new phone that the police had given him and his wallet, patting his trouser pocket. As the train slowed to almost a complete stop, he made the decision to jump.

Rico was used to achieving his goal at the first attempt, such was his skill set and precision and thoroughness. This is what made him popular with governments and drug barons and other shady organisations of that ilk. Non-traceable payments upon job completion was of benefit to hirers too. After coming to, Rico searched the train to no avail. Joe was gone.

*

Joe shuddered again as he remembered how close to death he had nearly come. Pat listened intently all the while in disbelief in what he was hearing.

"So, you've not got any protection now, then?"

"That's right. And I think he's still out there looking for me. I don't know who I can trust."

A tear ran down Joe's cheek as he recalled how young the two detectives were, who he assumed were now dead, and that their respective families were now fatherless and husbandless. Images came to mind of pictures shown to him on their phones of their families at the seaside with two small, beautiful children and another of two young girls and their mother in The Science Museum in London.

On seeing his new friend's plight, Pat felt helpless.

"Look, come and stay with me and my wife for the night and we'll get you to where you're going in the morning," offered Pat.

"That'd be great. Thanks."

"What happened to the detectives?"

"They must've been thrown off the train," surmised Joe. "I didn't see them again."

"Both of them?"

"I guess so. But how, I don't know. They were both stocky fellas and would've been hard to lift."

Mulling it over, Pat suddenly said, "Unless they were knocked out."

CHAPTER 9

Meanwhile, Alan Draper, a Senior Detective at Scotland Yard, was seated at his glass desk, checking up to date information on his biggest current case – a renowned reporter trusted by many MP's who had been entrusted with undisclosed secrets. The Home Office and MI5 were involved and even the most senior of police could not have details divulged to them. He was an older man, early 50's, with brown hair that was starting to grey and a beard to match. His suit, the best he could afford on his salary, was black with a white shirt and his tie, which his wife had bought for him last Christmas, had a grey-black pattern. His office was on the fifth floor overlooking the Thames with a view of the London Eye off to the left, but he seldom had time to sit there and admire it.

There was an urgent knocking on his office door. "Sir, Mitchell and Noonan have not reported in. We've tried calling them. Sounds like their phones are dead or switched off!" Baker said dramatically.

Sensing the worst, Alan immediately picked up the phone and dialled an internal number to his Superior to inform him of this latest development.

"Baker, gather a team for a train to Glasgow while I liaise with the authorities."

"Yes sir!"

As soon as Draper contacted the relevant authorities, the Home Office ordered an MI5 team to be rapidly assembled and brought up to speed on the events whilst another team created a time frame tracing movements and checking phone signals and their usage and CCTV footage in and around St Pancras. Every digital "fingerprint" — every transaction, wherever a pedestrian could have gone was intricately examined and investigated.

At the request of Draper's opposite number in MI5 and The Home Office, he found himself and his team scouring the wilderness, dogs straining at leashes relishing the new smells that were a delight to them. The co-operation between all departments trawling through video feeds and stills had resulted in an area being pin pointed to be searched for the missing detectives, and in turn, lead to the capture of their killer.

"Sir! Over here! I've found something," yelled a triumphant voice considering the circumstances.

Draper joined the member of his team that had called

him. Fearing the worst, he steeled himself for what was to be discovered. A bloodied piece of torn clothing caught around a sleeper of the track. Predicting the detective's trajectory from the train led to them to find a path of crushed foliage spattered with dried blood. And, judging by the way branches and leaves were crushed facing downhill away from the track embankment, could only come to one definitive conclusion.

The lifeless bodies of the two former detectives lay strewn forlornly and twisted amid the colourful bracken and ferns, devoid of colour. Staring, disbelieving eyes that still displayed the surprise, helplessness, and pleading that befell them. Limp like rag dolls with their heads turned at acute angles as they had fallen from the speeding train leaving a trail of blood, mucus and froth in their wake. A fresh offering to passing carnivorous animals and birds alike that no ravenous mammal could resist. Joe, however, was not with them.

Draper requested the lead local detective to go to the address which was the safe house. The town house was located on the outskirts of Corran and wasn't obvious to its purpose. Such was its ambiguity, local people were led to believe it was used as a holiday home, which police did to avoid raising suspicion. It was not disclosed to the local police due to its sensitivity. A report came back to Draper that the address was empty and there was no evidence to say it was inhabited.

CHAPTER 10

Scraping chairs, both Joe and Pat began making moves to leave. Looking over his shoulder as he put on his now somewhat dry coat, Joe said, "Just need to, you know."

"Right," replied Pat. "I'll meet you at the car."

Thomas and Ian both followed Pat outside of the pub. The torrential rain had stopped but the thick, heavy, dark clouds made it certain another downpour was imminent. Suddenly, a growing feeling of dread consumed them both as they noticed a man standing in the shadows, holding a cigarette. The creak of the pub door caused both Thomas and Ian to turn their heads in time to see Joe exit and head towards the car. The shadowy man seemed to melt into the brickwork. Thomas and Ian stiffened. The assassin had tracked them to the pub!

Pat had the car running while he waited for Joe. Methodical as always, Rico stood in an unlit part of the car park, puffing on his cigarette. He patiently watched as Joe climbed in and the taxi pulled away, turning left. As soon as the car was out of sight, Rico took a tool out of his back pack, smashing a back window of an SUV from the car park. He reached an arm around to open the door, brushed the broken glass off the seat and climbed in. Hot wiring the car, he took off after them.

Having studied the mountainous terrain with its twisty turning roads and absence of guard rails in many places, the sheer drops helped Rico develop his plan.

"We need to warn them!" whispered Ian.

"We can't, remember. They can't hear or see us and we can't change what has already happened. It can only play out," whispered Thomas in reply.

Suddenly the scenery changed once again, followed by the whooshing sound. They found themselves on a high mountain road, looking down towards village lights in the distance.

First, they heard the noise. The noise of car engines racing, accelerating, then tyres squealing as they struggled to grip the surface of the road and the sound of metal on metal crunching. As the two cars came into view, Pat's taxi was in front, closely followed by another vehicle being driven by the man who emerged from the shadows. The assassin's car continuously rammed into what was left of the rear bumper of Pat's taxi, causing it to veer from one side of the road to the other.

With an impending sense of doom and foreboding, the

pursuit felt interminable. Pat felt so helpless. "Go faster!" Joe screamed. Pat obeyed. The car rounded a bend and a final shunt caused the taxi to lose control. It careered onto the other side of the road, picking up speed as it launched over the crash barrier and hurtled down the side of the embankment, somersaulting through the air until finally landing on its roof.

The stranger in the attacking car came to a halt by the broken barrier, quickly climbed out to survey the wreckage. Using his torch to light the way, he clambered down the rocky embankment to check for survivors. Plumes of charcoal grey smoke were billowing from under the smashed in bonnet. The unmistakable smell of petrol fumes hung in the air. The assassin knew he didn't have long before the whole car would become a giant ball of fire. The side facing him after his descent was the driver's. He could see the driver slumped over the wheel and lifeless, covered in blood. Looking through the smashed window, he could see the passenger side was empty. Pulling his gun, he carefully made his way around to the other side of the car. There he found Joe, still alive but barely, lying on his back, a short distance from the vehicle, blood soaking through his clothes and matting his hair, crying in pain.

Thomas and Ian could hear Joe pleading for his life.

"Please don't kill me! I'll give you the documents you want," begged Joe, pointing to the inside pocket of his coat.

The assassin walked over and pulled out the envelope.

"Thanks," said the assassin, who raised his gun and promptly shot Joe in the head. Before turning to crawl his way back up the side of the road, he turned back towards the car, which now had bright yellow and orange flames licking at the crisp night air and tossed the envelope into the fire.

*

The next morning Draper and his team accompanied the local police to a road traffic accident. He had to report this to his opposite number at MI5. On retracing the deceased's footsteps, it became rapidly apparent that no one had overheard the two gentlemen in the pub. And so, under a direct order from high up in MI5, this case of national security was hushed up.

CHAPTER 11

Breathless and shocked, Thomas and Ian quickly came out of Thomas's episode. Now panting hard, Thomas released Ian's forearm and shakily reached for his glass of water. Ian did likewise. A stunned silence ensued for several minutes. Ian opened a window, loosened his tie and took large gulps of fresh mountain air. He had never experienced anything like this. He slowly realised what a burden it was for Thomas to carry.

Breaking the silence, Ian had questions. "How do you cope with everything you see?"

"I must admit it was hard at first but this has been a part of my life for so long now. Talking to people like you really helps me," replied Thomas.

"So, this national security secret. It stayed secret from the public then?"

"Yeah. That's right. Joe never got to write his story. It died with him."

"But how did you know and see all this?"

"Joe appeared to me. I felt his presence. His sadness and regret. I can pick up their feelings. They reach out to me. It's like these spirits can talk to me and share pieces of their lives," explained Thomas.

"So, do you know what this secret was?" asked Ian cautiously.

"Yes, to some extent, but not all the details. I don't want *or* need to know too much. Let's just say that someone high up in the government who retired early due to ill health was really fit as a fiddle but was covertly arrested and put on trial for sharing knowledge which should have remained secret," explained Thomas.

"Wow! No wonder it was hushed up," exclaimed Ian. "Was this secret the reason Joe made contact with you then?"

"Not directly, but he wanted to make sure Detective Draper had enough of the story so he knew what really happened to his men and to Pat. He knew I'd be able to speak to the police and be believed, as I had worked with them before."

Thomas looked visibly relieved to have unburdened himself. What felt like a huge passage of time, appeared to have only been forty minutes. Ian got up and shook hands with Thomas as he said goodbye to him at the door.

Turning around, Ian mopped his fevered brow and

took a breather to take stock of what had just unravelled as he gazed out of a window.

EPILOGUE – TEN YEARS AGO

The gentle heat from the radiant yellow sun shone high in the sky. Fluffy white clouds floated effortlessly across the majestic backdrop of the Scottish foothills.

A young Thomas and Jemma were out enjoying another of their rambling sightseeing tours. In the distance, they could hear a humdrum of activity and were curious as to what was happening. Steadily, they made their way towards the voices.

As they were getting closer, a large white tent came into view, guarded by a young male police officer. Other police personnel were scattered about, deep in conversation with each other and what looked like a forensic team.

"Sorry sir, but you'll have to turn back," said the young constable.

"What's happened here?" enquired Thomas, taking in the scene.

"I'm afraid I can't say sir, police business."

Suddenly Thomas became motionless, as if in a trance, and stared out through the forensic team at work. The constable was looking at Thomas's bizarre behaviour.

"It's alright," stated Jemma and began explaining who Thomas was and his previous work with the police.

Thomas walked off to the side, to Joe, who no one else could hear or see, and began what appeared to everyone else, a one-sided conversation.

About The Author

I was born in 1969 in Sidcup, Kent. My father was a Chief Inspector in the Metropolitan Police and my mother was a housewife. I grew up and went to school in Bexley, Kent. My love of writing started from a young age, as I was always reading and had a creative mind. Teachers were impressed with my writing and moved me up to higher English groups. My writing was exhibited at the school.

I am married to a teacher and have one son. I was a highly qualified independent driving instructor for 15 years. During this time, I studied hypnotherapy. I have always been writing stories and poetry for pleasure but over the past 6 years, I took up writing in earnest in the hope of achieving publication which has always been my ambition. I draw inspiration from the people in my life and some of my own personal experiences.

www.blossomspringpublishing.com